I would like to dedicate this book to the **Super Smart Girls.** I wish every club member much success, peace, and happiness. You are the leaders of tomorrow, and may God direct your path.

Angelica L. Rodriguez

Kaitny Stroman

Hannah Reason

Mary Catherine Reason

Nia Scott

Jada Mosley

Ka'Maria Johnson

Passion Johnson

The Super Smart Girls Club of Simpsonville,

South Carolina

www.mascotbooks.com

Shayla Sweet and Her Magical Pen

For more information, please contact:
Mascot Books
620 Herndon Parkway, Suite 320
Herndon, VA 20170
info@mascotbooks.com

Library of Congress Control Number: 2020901256

CPSIA Code: PRTWP0720A
ISBN-13: 978-1-64307-356-9

Printed in South Korea

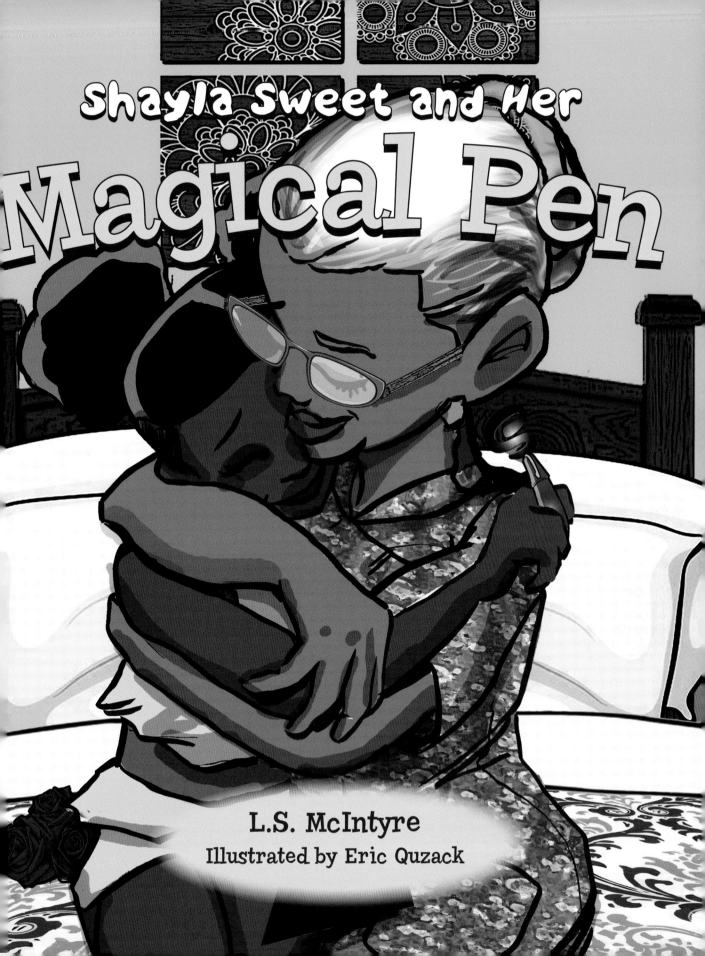

Shayla Sweet and Her
Magical Pen

L.S. McIntyre

Illustrated by Eric Quzack

Wow! It's summer break, and I am so happy to be at Nani's house. All I have to do today is make my bed and clean my room.

"Shayla, breakfast is ready!" yells Nani.

"Coming!" I reply. "I just have to grab my magic pen and pad!"

"Good Morning, Nani," I say. This breakfast is so yummy!

"I have to write this down before I forget," I say to myself.

"Shayla, eat your breakfast and put that magic pen down!" Nani yells.

"Okay Nani," I say.

"Shayla, go outside and pick me
ten roses," says Nani.
"Okay Nani," I say.

I go outside to the garden and pick
three roses. Then I start writing with
my magic pen.

Nani comes outside. "Shayla, what are you doing?" she asks.

"I'm writing, Nani," I say. I love to
write with my magic pen.

"Well, go inside to the kitchen and get me a vase for these flowers," Nani says.
"Okay Nani," I reply.

I start writing with my magic pen again.

"Shayla, what are you doing?" Nani asks.

"Nani, I'm writing with my magic pen," I say.

"Shayla, please go to your room and take a nap," Nani says.

Nani waits a few minutes before coming into my room to check on me.

"Oh no!" yells Nani. "Shayla, what are you doing?"

"I'm writing with my magic pen," I say.

Nani says, "Shayla, I asked you to eat your breakfast, and you didn't. I asked you to pick ten flowers, and you didn't. I asked you to get me a vase, and you didn't.

I asked you to take a nap, and you didn't. So, what are you writing about with your magic pen?"

"I'm writing a story about how much love is needed in the world."

"Well then, tell me about your story," Nani says.

I start to read aloud. "There is so much love that is needed in the world. People are hungry and need food to eat. People are thirsty and need clean water to drink. People are sad and need some happiness. People are homeless and need a place to call home. Some children are without parents and need a family. And some people are without God and need His grace and mercy to shine."

there is so much love that is needed
in the world
people are hungry and need food to eat
people are thirsty and need clean water
to drink. people are sad and need some
happiness
people are homeless and need
a place to call home.
some children are without parents and need
a family.
people are without god and need his grace
and mercy to shine

"Wow!" Nani exclaims. "Shayla Sweet, you keep writing with that magic pen of yours, and you just might discover how to **spread love that will shine on everyone!** I love you."

"I love you, too," I say. I'm glad she likes my story. I wonder what I'll write about tomorrow.

Author L.S. McIntyre was raised in Brooklyn, New York. She is the proud mother of three children and is the founder/director of the Super Smart Girl's Club, a literacy-based nonprofit organization designed to mentor and motivate young girls ages 2-18. L.S. McIntyre takes pride in her books of positivity and inspiration.